A MOTHER'S *Heart*

HAPPY MOTHER'S DAY

Bethlehem Presbyterian Church

May 11, 2003

A MOTHER'S

Heart

ELLYN SANNA

BARBOUR
PUBLISHING, INC.
Uhrichsville, Ohio

© MCMXCIX by Barbour Publishing, Inc.

ISBN 1-57748-431-2

Published by Barbour Publishing, Inc., P.O. Box 719, Uhrichsville, OH 44683 http://www.barbourbooks.com

ecpa Member of the
Evangelical Christian
Publishers Association

Printed in the United States of America.

GOD'S MIRRORS

Mother is the name for God in the lips
and hearts of little children.
—*William Makepeace Thackeray*

∽

"As one whom his mother comforteth,
so will I comfort you."
—*Isaiah 66:13*

∽

God loves us the way a good mother loves—
totally, unconditionally, with a nurturing and
ever-present care. In fact, as mothers, our love for
our children is only a dim reflection of the love
God has for His people.

GOD'S IMAGE IN MOTHERHOOD

When the apostle Paul preached to the people of
Athens, he told them, "You have been worshiping

him without knowing who he is, and now I wish to tell you about him. He is the God who made the world and everything in it. . . . He himself gives life and breath to everything, and he satisfies every need there is. . . . His purpose in all of this was that the nations should seek after God and perhaps feel their way toward him and find him—though he is not far from any one of us. For in him we live and move and exist. . . . 'We are his offspring' " (Acts 17:23–25, 27–28 NLT).

In other words, Paul is saying a mother's relationship with her children is a perfect example of God's love for us, whether we know His name or not. Paul doesn't explicitly mention mothers, of course—but mothers are the ones who give life, the ones who constantly meet their children's physical needs from the moment of conception. During pregnancy, the baby literally lives and moves and has its being within the mother. And I believe that Paul is drawing the analogy between that intimate, physical dependency which the baby has on its mother, and our own relationship with God. Our nurturing, life-giving God offers us a constant and ever-present love—like a mother.

Fatherhood is the metaphor we usually use to relate to God—and obviously, the father image is one that illumines for many the power and love we find in God's nature. But God has given us glimpses of Himself in all of our human relationships. Christ is also the Baby, the innocent Child, and He is also our Brother and our Friend. Even the relationship between animal and human shows us something of God's love for us—think about the Good Shepherd. Any pet lover experiences a wonderful metaphor for the care and interest and delight that God feels for us. Given all that, it only makes sense that we also find God in motherhood.

The prophet Isaiah spoke of God as a mother who holds her baby on her lap. He compared the tie between God and His people to that between a nursing mother and her child—and we mothers who nursed our babies know just how intense that tie is. Christ Himself said He longed to gather Jerusalem to Him, like a mother hen gathers her chicks. He could have said, "I long to fight all your enemies, the way a rooster will defend his brood"—but instead He used another metaphor, one that shows Him to be nurturing, protective, and longing for closeness the way a mother longs to snuggle her children.

In Him we live and move and have our being. What does that mean? For those of us mothers who have been pregnant, think about what the experience is like. Wherever you go, no matter what, the baby is with you, enclosed in your flesh, cushioned by your body. You are so close to your baby that it probably doesn't even know you're there, because you are its world. Your body supplies its every need. Without any effort on the baby's part, it is enclosed in love, nurtured at every moment.

And as Paul said to the Athenians—that's how it is with God. We're so used to thinking of ourselves as struggling toward God; we use concepts like fighting and exercising and mountain climbing to think of the spiritual journey—and yes, we need those metaphors, and Paul himself made use of them in other places. But meanwhile, all the while, we're simply surrounded by God, without any effort whatsoever on our part. In Him we live and move and have our being—He is so close to us, so intimately connected to our lives, that we cannot even comprehend how dependent we are on Him. As Paul says later in his letter to the Romans, we can *never* be separated from the love of God. We are enclosed in it, just as a baby is in its mother's womb.

Because God's love is reflected in ours, our children will learn about God simply through motherhood's love. Oh, we need to teach our children about God and His Word, we need to read them Bible stories and pray with them, answer their questions and take them to church. We need to live in such a way that they'll see what it means to be a Christian. But on a much more basic level, they'll understand about a God who always hears, because when they were babies we responded to their cries. They'll be able to have faith in a God who meets their needs, because we saw that they never went hungry. God's strength and tenderness will be real to them, because they caught a glimpse of it in our love from the time they were born.

So, mothers, never let the world tell you that what you do is not important. Remember, when you rock your babies and sing a lullaby, your arms and voice are God's. When you do load after load of dirty diapers, and then grass-stained play clothes, and finally school clothes smeared with ketchup and chocolate pudding, remember, your hands are God's hands. And when you love your children unconditionally, all the way from colic to adolescent rebellion, you are loving with God's love. Through you, He will imprint Himself on your children's hearts. The Holy Spirit will draw them throughout their entire lives, so that one day on the foundation you laid they may build an adult faith in Jesus Christ.[1]

∽

The soul can split the sky in two,
And let the face of God shine through.
—*Edna St. Vincent Millay*

∽

"My soul doth magnify the Lord,
and my spirit hath rejoiced in God my Saviour."
—*Luke 1:46–47*

∽

As mothers, we can be comforted that not only does God love our children far more than we will ever be able, but He loves us in the same way. We should also be challenged to commit our love for our children to God, to be used by Him as a vehicle to touch our children's lives. This sort of committed love is like a lens that will catch the Spirit's light and magnify it in our children's lives—and as Edna St. Vincent Millay said, this sort of holy love can "split the sky in two," allowing our children to catch a glimpse of God's shining face.

∽

Be thou my Sun, my selfishness destroy,
Thy atmosphere of Love be all my joy;
Thy Presence be my sunshine ever bright,
My soul the little mote that lives but in
    Thy light.

        —*Gerhard Tersteegen*

∽

There are two ways of spreading light: to be the
candles or the mirror that reflects it.
        —*Edith Wharton*

∽

Dear God, thank You for Your limitless love. As much as I love my children, I know You love them infinitely more. Please take my flawed, human love for my children and use it for Your glory. Let me be a clear mirror that reflects Your light; help me to magnify You. Amen.

FLAME-KINDLERS,
SEED-PLANTERS,
WEALTH-GIVERS

"I have been reminded of your sincere faith, which first lived in your grandmother Lois and in your mother Eunice and, I am persuaded, now lives in you also."

—*2 Timothy 1:5 (NIV)*

∽

From women's eyes this doctrine I derive:
They sparkle still the right Promethean
   fire;
They are the books, the arts, the academes,
That show, contain, and nourish all the
   world.

—*William Shakespeare*

∽

*As mothers, we have an awesome opportunity:
the chance to plant seeds, kindle fires, and impart*

a legacy of wealth. These seeds may not germinate for many years, sometimes not until after our own death; the fires may only smolder until our children reach adulthood, when suddenly, the Spirit's breath fans them into life. But we can be confident that the things our children learn from us of God and His Son will be a permanent part of their hearts, enriching their lives and eventually their children's lives, an eternal heritage from one generation to the next.

Maternal Solicitude

A mother's love!—how sweet the name!
 The holiest, purest, tenderest flame
That kindles from above;
 Within a heart of earthly mould
As much of heaven as heart can hold
 Nor through eternity grows cold—
That is a mother's love.

—*Montgomery*

"The future destiny of a child," said Napoleon, "is always the work of its mother." She will give it its character, and its character will determine its future life. As the child runs about her in its earliest years, every glance, look, tone of voice, and action sinks into the heart and memory, and is presently reproduced in its own little life and its many child-ish actions; and then, as life goes on, those tones and looks and actions are reproduced in maturity, and are not obliterated when old age comes on. Every stage in its life gives the impress and motive to the next, so that the last stage of all partakes something of the first. It is thus in this sense true that the child is father to the man. The first and obviously the most important work of education is the development of the faculties which lie latent in the child, waiting to be unfolded by judicious exercise. The constant and endeared companion of the child is the mother; to her, both by nature and opportunity, is committed the charge of unrolling its faculties, and of further encouraging it in the pursuit and attainment of knowledge. If she is mean and contracted in her purposes, selfish and passion-ate, ignorant and ill-disciplined, it is only natural that her offspring should grow up mean, passionate, and ignorant also. She forms a climate in which her little one breathes, creates the circumstances by which it is surrounded, which temper and tone its mind, which give the impetus to its dispositions and the formations of its habits.

Did it begin when the parental ear was delighted with the lisping of the first word? Long before that; for there is a language earlier than speech, and which speech can never express—the language of looks— the communion of sympathy between the world with-out and the world within. Did it begin the first time its untrained foot touched the earth? Long before that; by that time many a step had been taken, involving future consequences of infinite importance. Did it begin with the first smile that dimpled its cheek and beamed in its eye? Earlier than that—so early that in afteryears its memory can never go far enough back to date its commencement; earlier than the moment of the first maternal smile and embrace, for these only contributed to promote it. And all the impressions which it received from that period—and probably it does receive impressions through every subsequent moment—all these are part of the materials out of which its future character is to be formed, all these are vital seeds, some of which will be bearing their appropriate fruit ten thousand ages hence. [1]

∽

> Who ran to help me when I fell,
>   And would some pretty story tell,
> Or kiss the place to make it well?
>   My mother.

—Ann Taylor

∽

Sometimes we do not have the chance to love our children from birth—and yet our adopted children and stepchildren can still find their hearts enriched by the spiritual wealth they receive from us. It is never too late to plant seeds for God, for no matter how late our children come into our lives, God can still touch them through us, just as He does Dan in this story by Louisa May Alcott.

A MOTHER'S INFLUENCE

Mrs. Jo had a way of flitting about the house at night, to shut the windows if the wind grew chilly, to draw mosquito curtains over Teddy, or look after Tommy, who occasionally walked in his sleep. The least noise waked her, and as she often heard imaginary robbers, cats, and conflagrations, the doors stood open all about, so her quick ear caught the sound of Dan's little moans, and she was up in a minute. He was just giving his hot pillow a despairing thump when a light came glimmering from the hall, and Mrs. Jo crept in, looking like a droll ghost, with her hair in a great knob on the top of her head, and a long gray dressing-gown tailing behind her.

"Are you in pain, Dan?"

"It's pretty bad; but I didn't mean to wake you."

"I'm a sort of owl, always flying about at night. Yes, your foot is like fire; the bandages must be wet again," and away flapped the maternal owl for more cooling stuff, and a great mug of ice water.

"Oh, that's *so* nice!" sighed Dan, as the wet bandages went on again, and a long draught of water cooled his thirsty throat.

"There, now, sleep your best, and don't be frightened if you see me again, for I'll slip down by and by, and give your foot another sprinkle."

As she spoke, Mrs. Jo stooped to turn the pillow and smooth the bedclothes, when, to her great surprise, Dan put his arm around her neck, drew her face down to his, and kissed her, with a broken "Thank you, ma'am," which said more than the most eloquent speech could have done. . . . She kissed the brown cheek half hidden on the pillow, as if ashamed of that little touch of tenderness, and left him, saying, what he long remembered, "You are my boy now, and if you choose you can make me proud and glad to say so. . . . You shall have all the help we can give you now, and I hope to teach you how to behave yourself in the best way. Have you forgotten what Father Bhaer told you. . .about wanting to be good, and asking God to help you?"

"No, ma'am," very low.

"Do you try that way still?"

"No, ma'am," lower still.

"Will you do it every night to please me?"

"Yes, ma'am," very soberly.

"I shall depend on it, and I think I shall know if you are faithful to your promise, for these things always show to people who believe in them, though not a word is said. . . ."

Dan lay in his pleasant room wide awake, thinking new thoughts, feeling new hopes and desires stirring in his boyish heart, for two good angels had entered in: love and gratitude began the work which time and effort were to finish; and with an earnest wish to keep his first promise, Dan folded his hands together in the darkness. . . .

"Please, God bless everyone, and help me to be good." [2]

No man is poor who has had a godly mother.
> —*Abraham Lincoln*

∽

A rich child often sits in a poor mother's lap.
> —*Danish proverb*

∽

There is in every true woman's heart a spark of heavenly fire, which lies dormant in the broad daylight of prosperity, but which kindles up and beams and blazes in the dark hour of adversity.
> —*Washington Irving*

∽

A mother is not a person to lean on,
but a person to make leaning unnecessary.
> —*Dorothy Canfield Fisher*

∽

Sometimes our responsibilities to our children seem too awesome: We must not only keep them clean and safe and healthy, but we must also be responsible for planting spiritual seeds, lighting holy fires, passing along God's wealth. We must take care of them, nurture them, meet their needs— and at the same time we must enable them to grow up strong, dependent on God rather than ourselves. Sometimes it seems too much to ask of one busy and all too human mother.

Before we start to stumble under this load,

though, we need to remember that really, our only responsibility is to God: to be the sort of women He calls us to be. He will take care of the rest. As we live our lives in right relationship with God, His Spirit will be the One who plants the seeds; He will be the One who drops a spark into the tinder of our children's hearts; and He will be the One who uses our conse- crated lives to pass along the bounty of His riches.

∽

"Believe in the Lord Jesus, and you will be saved—you and your household."
—*Acts 16:31 (NIV)*

∽

Dear Lord, please use me to make my children strong. Teach them of Yourself through me—and may they remember what they learn their whole lives long. You know how many times I fail, You know how selfish and confused I can be some- times—so use me in spite of myself. And one day in heaven, my children and I will give You all the glory. Amen.

MARRIAGE & LOVE

"Intreat me not to leave thee, or to return from following after thee: for whither thou goest, I will go;
and where thou lodgest, I will lodge: thy people
shall be my people, and thy God my God."

—*Ruth 1:16*

Take love when love is given,
But never think to find it
A sure escape from sorrow
Or a complete repose.

—*Sara Teasdale*

I like not only to be loved,
but also to be told that I am loved.

—*George Eliot*
(Marian Evans Cross)

Married love is a wonderful gift from God. In the intimacy between husband and wife, we see revealed yet another aspect of God's love for us. As wonderful as this love is, however, we need to remember that only God loves perfectly. When we expect our husbands to be perfect, we are bound to be frustrated, just as Katy is in the story that follows. Throw in some of the irritations that often accompany married life (in Katy's case, unsympathetic in-laws), and we, like Katy, may find ourselves feeling disillusioned with married love. Sometimes, though, the solution lies in understanding the differences between our husband's emotional makeup and our own.

MARRIED TRIALS

Things are even worse than I expected. Ernest evidently looked at me with his father's eyes (and this father has got the jaundice, or something) and certainly is cooler toward me than he was before he went home. Martha still declines eating more than enough to keep body and soul together and sits at the table with the air of a martyr. Her father lives on crackers and stewed prunes; and when he has eaten them, fixes his melancholy eyes on me, watching every mouthful I consume with an air of plaintive regret that I will consume so much unwholesome food.

Then Ernest positively spends less time with

me than ever and sits in his office reading and writing nearly every evening.

Yesterday I came home from an exhilarating walk and a charming call at Aunty's and at the dinner table gave a lively account of some of the children's exploits. Nobody laughed, and nobody made any response; and after dinner Ernest took me aside and said, kindly enough, but still said it, "My little wife must be careful how she runs on in my father's presence. He has great dread of everything that might be thought levity."

Then all the vials of my wrath exploded and went off.

"Yes, I see how it is," I cried passionately. "You and your father and your sister have got a box about a foot square that you want to squeeze me into. I have seen it ever since they came. And I can tell you it will take more than the three of you to do it. There was no harm in what I said—none, whatever. If you only married me for the sake of screwing me down and freezing me up, why didn't you tell me so before it was too late?"

Ernest stood looking at me like one staring at a problem he had got to solve and didn't know where to begin.

"I am very sorry," he said. "I thought you would be glad to have me give you this little hint. Of course I want you to appear your very best before my father and sister."

"My very best is my real self," I cried. "If your father doesn't like me, I wish he would go away and not come here putting notions into your head and making you as cold and hard as stone. Mother liked to have me 'run on' as you call it, and I wish I had stayed with her all my life."

"Do you mean," he asked, very gravely, "that you really wish that?"

"No," I said, "I don't mean it," for his husky, troubled voice brought me to my senses. "All I mean is that I love you so dearly, and you keep my heart feeling so hungry and restless. . . . I never dreamed you would disappoint me so!"

"Will you stop crying and listen to me?" he said.

But I could not stop. The floods of the great deep were broken up at last, and I had to cry. . . .

Ernest walked up and down in silence. Oh, if I could have cried on his breast and felt he loved and pitied me!

At last, I grew quieter and he came and sat by me.

"This has come upon me like a thunderclap," he said. "I did not know I kept your heart hungry. . . . And I took it for granted that my wife, with her high-toned, heroic character, would sustain me in every duty and welcome my father and sister into our home. I do not know what I can do now. Shall I send them away?"

"No, no!" I cried. "Only be good to me, Ernest, only love me, only look at me with your own eyes, not with other people's. You knew I had faults when you married me; I never tried to conceal them."

"And did you fancy I had none myself?" he asked.

"N–o," I replied. "I saw no faults in you. . .you

spoke so beautifully one night at an evening meeting."

"Speaking beautifully is little to the purpose unless one lives beautifully," he said sadly. ". . . Are you to wear your life out because I have not your frantic way of loving, and am I to be made weary of mine because I cannot satisfy you? . . .I do love you, and that more than you know. But you would not have me leave my work and spend my whole time telling you so?"

"You know I am not so silly," I cried. "It is not fair, it is not right to talk as if I were. I ask for nothing unreasonable. I only want those little daily assurances of your affection that I should suppose would be spontaneous if you felt at all toward me as I do to you."

"The fact is," he returned, "I am absorbed in my work. . . . Katy," he said, "if you can once make up your mind that I am an undemonstrative man, not all fire and fury and ecstasy as you are, yet loving you with all my heart, however it may seem, I think you will spare yourself much needless pain— and spare me also."

"But I want you to be demonstrative," I persisted. . . .

By this time there was a call for Ernest—it is a wonder there had not been forty—and he went.

I feel as heartsore as ever. [1]

∾

An ideal wife is any woman who
has an ideal husband.
—*Booth Tarkington*

As unto the bow the cord is,
　　So unto the man is woman;
Though she bends him, she obeys him,
　　Though she draws him, yet she follows;
Useless each without the other.
　　　　　　　—Henry Wadsworth Longfellow

～

Marriage, to women as to men, must be a luxury,
not a necessity; an incident of life, not all of it.
　　　　　　　—Susan Brownell Anthony

～

We want our marriages to be joyful and loving —but sometimes we feel frustrated and hurt. Instead of expecting our husbands to meet all our needs, though, we should be relying on God for strength and understanding. This is the best way to make our marriages be all they can be.

MARRIED PEACE:
FORGET THE FAIRY TALES

Sometimes I don't like being married. Oh, I do love my husband. And I've made promises—promises I intend to keep. But those promises don't magically wipe away the frustration and conflict that sometimes arise between husband and wife. As Christians we're committed to the permanence of marriage, but how do we learn to reconcile the everyday differences that trouble our home's peace? Whatever happened to "happily ever after"?

Since childhood we may have heard stories of conflict *before* marriage, but in the fairy tales, once two people marry, they are happy forevermore, end of story. That fairy-tale image of love explains why we sometimes doubt our love. After all, if we're not happy, then something must be wrong.

Those thoughts nibble at the underside of even the strongest Christian marriages, particularly during the early years, before experiences give greater perspective. Before we learn that marriage is hard work.

By definition, marriage requires that two distinct entities become one. No matter how much in love we are, no matter how committed as Christians we are, making one thing out of two separate things is not an easy task. R. C. Sproul once said that "If you imagined your mother married to your father-in-law, and your father married your to mother-in-law, you'd have a good picture of the dynamics of marriage." I dearly love both my parents and my in-laws, but that quote always makes me smile, for it creates an image in my mind of two preposterous unions.

I don't smile nearly as wide, though, when the quote's truth becomes plain in my own marriage. A peaceful union is hard to achieve. Oneness is not something that can happen overnight. The marriage ceremony does not erase the differences between husband and wife, nor does it cancel their selfish natures. Married unity requires instead an acceptance that conflict is bound to occur; it also requires a commitment to ongoing reconciliation—for a lifetime.

The writer of James has simple and practical wisdom for achieving this lifelong reconciliation: "Be quick to listen, slow to speak and slow to become angry" (James 1:19 NIV). This is the kind of advice I need to post on my refrigerator, hang above my dryer, stick to my bathroom mirror. . .until it becomes a permanent part of my thoughts. I need to wear it inside my heart daily, moment by moment, for it requires a radical shift in my outlook.

James's words are similar to this prayer of Francis of Assisi: "Lord, make me an instrument of Thy peace. . . . Grant that I may not so much seek. . . to be understood as to understand, to be loved as to love. . . ." Both James and Francis are talking about a total reversal in the way we approach others, a kind of turning ourselves inside out.

Instead of looking at how our spouse fails to give to us, we should be looking for ways to give to him. Instead of feeling frustrated because our spouse doesn't understand us, we should concentrate on listening better, so that we can understand.

But sometimes we feel too hurt, too tired, too frustrated; we don't want to listen, we want to be heard. Those are usually the times when an unexpected crisis—like financial worries, illness, or problems with a child—sends married partners reeling in opposite directions. When we handle life's catastrophes in separate, sometimes conflicting ways, our "happily ever after" seems gone forever.

Love alone can't always reach far enough to span the dark times. After all, if I'm desperate to be heard, to have my own anguish acknowledged and comforted, how can I listen and give to anyone else, even someone I love as much as I do my husband? Once again, those fairy tales cloud our vision. Despite what romantic stories tell us, a married couple is not a self-sufficient unit.

When I feel hurt and frustrated because my husband's not meeting some need of mine, I remind myself of something a friend told me. "Suppose," she said, "you were out of bread, and so you went to the closest store to buy some. The closest store, though, just happened to be a hardware store, and of course they didn't have any bread. 'But I really need bread,' you'd plead. You might even cry, and then you'd get angry, and storm around shouting that they were being unreasonable not to give you what you truly, legitimately needed. But they wouldn't give you any bread. They couldn't. They didn't have any."

That's what we're like when we expect our spouse to meet our every need. They can't. They're not God. Only He can satisfy our every need—and sometimes, He supplies our needs through other sources than our husbands.

We're being just as unrealistic when we expect our love to carry too great a load. Paul says that faith, hope, and love are the three things that last (1 Corinthians 13:13), and we talk a great deal about faith and love. We tend, however, to skim over hope, as though it were somehow not quite as practical as the other two, not essential to our daily lives. In fact, hope is what carries us forward, even when our love seems dry and dead. Hope is the bridge that gets us over the dark times. It's what keeps us believing in the future, no matter what the present looks like.

Hopelessness refuses to believe that God can change us, and it closes the door to the possibilities of the future. The hope that Paul speaks of is not a cheery, optimistic attitude that somehow the best will always happen. Instead, the bridge of hope is anchored firmly on one side by our love and on the other by our faith in Christ; it spans the distance between the two.

James says, "Confess your sins to each other and pray for each other so that you may be healed. The prayer of a righteous man is powerful and effective" (5:16 NIV). In other words, in our marriage—as in all the rest of our life—our hope is in the Lord. When we make room for prayer's power to work in the midst of our conflict, who knows what miracles of peace and reconciliation we will see? [2]

∽

Talk not of wasted affection;
affection never was wasted.
—*Henry Wadsworth Longfellow*

Things base and vile, holding no quantity,
Love can transpose to form and dignity.
Love looks not with the eyes, but with the
    mind,
And therefore is winged Cupid painted
    blind.

               —William Shakespeare

Our culture leads us to have high expectations for marriage. We expect the romance to last forever —and usually what we mean is that we want to be complimented and petted; we want our husbands to make us feel excited and comforted, attractive and desirable. Romance is a part of marriage, even the longest and oldest marriages—but a more important part is commitment. Commitment is what will get us past those dry times when we don't feel excited or attractive; when instead we may feel angry and bored.

Our husbands are only human. We cannot expect them to meet our needs all the time—any more than they can expect us to meet theirs all the time. Instead, marriage is a partnership between two people who are committed to loving each other forever, through hard times and easy, through excitement and boredom. The stability and constancy of married love reflects God's love for us—and within marriage's boundaries we truly find one of life's greatest joys.

How do I love thee? Let me count the ways. . . .
　　If God choose, I shall but love thee
　　　　better after death.
—Elizabeth Barrett Browning

∽

How many loved your moments of glad
　　grace,
And loved your beauty with love false
　　or true,
But one man loved the pilgrim soul in you,
And loved the sorrows of your changing
　　face.
—William Butler Yeats

∽

Dear Jesus, thank You for my husband. Help me to be a good friend to him, as well as a good wife. Remind me to worry more about understanding than being understood—and thank You that I can rely on You to understand, even when my husband doesn't, just as I can depend on You for all the comfort and strength I need. Please make our marriage truly an image of Your love for Your church. May Your Spirit inhabit our marriage and fill it with Your joy. Amen.

HOME

It is not our exalted feelings, it is our sentiments
that build the necessary home.
                                    —*Elizabeth Bowen*

∽

*Our homes are the private spaces that belong
uniquely to our own families. They are havens of
security that bear the stamp of our personalities—
and they are far more than four walls and a roof. As
the following selection indicates, what makes a
house a home has more to do with our attitude and
behaviors—and very little to do with things like
curtains and carpets, landscaping and square foot-
age of living space.*

HOME SINS

Let anyone who claims the name of Christ renounce
all family sin. I am talking about a sort of private
house-sin—a sin that never appears in public places,

but that only comes out in the privacy of our own homes. David, that whole and healthy man, was aware of this, for he said that he would act with wisdom, in a perfect way; in fact, he said, "I will lead a life of integrity in my own home" (Psalm 101:2 NLT).

Many people act like saints when they are out in public, but at home, when they give way to this house-sin, they are more like devils. This is the sort of sin that meets the husband and wife at their door; it keeps them from taking so much as a step inside without them beginning to argue with each other. Obviously, they are not acting much like partners in grace. Wives and husbands should hand this grace back and forth between them. The husband should love his wife just as Christ does His church, and the wife should return his love, just as the church returns her Savior's love. As the Bible says, "Submit to one another out of reverence for Christ" (Ephesians 5:21 NIV) and "You husbands must give honor to your wives. Treat her with understanding as you live together. . .she is your equal partner in God's gift of new life" (1 Peter 3:7 NLT). Until your marriage is built on this sort of love and respect, your house-sin will flourish within the privacy of your home. But God sees within the walls of your house just as well as He sees your behavior in public, and the sin that you show no one except your spouse will be revealed on the day of judgment, as openly as any public sin.

In fact, the way you act at home tells more about

the true nature of your mind and emotions than does the way you act when you are out in public on your best behavior. If my life depended on me making an accurate judgment about a person's life, I would base my judgment not on that person's public reputation but on the intimate domestic behaviors that tell so much more about a person's true self.

Our public Christian behavior is like our best clothes that we put on to go out in—when we come home, we take them off and hang them in the closet. But what we are at home is who we really are. We have to be a Christian in many arenas of life: the public world, our homes, and our most intimate interior selves, the secret rooms in our hearts that we share with no one. The way we are at home, as well as the way we are in that secret space inside ourselves, that is where we show our true selves. Maybe the world cannot see us—but our families can, and so can the angels.

The people in my home are God's special gift to me. That is why my goal should always be to live my religion in their presence, live with a life filled with the power of godliness rather than the sin of self. That is what God wants of me, and this is what will make Him happy. The Lord said of Abraham, "I have singled him out so that he will direct his sons and their families to keep the way of the LORD and do what is right and just. Then I will do for him all that I have promised" (Genesis 18:19 NLT). The Lord will do the same for us. [1]

"Lord, through all the generations
you have been our home!"
—*Psalm 90:1 (NLT)*

❧

The above verse from the Ninetieth Psalm indicates what our true home really is: God Himself! The security, pleasure, and comfort that we find in our homes are only one more reflection of God's nature, another way we can catch a glimpse of the God we love. Most of us love our homes—but when we consider that they are actually small reflections of God, then the word "home" takes on even more meaning.

Sacred Places

Our homes are sacred places. They should speak to us of God just as clearly as our churches do. Judaism is more apt to remember the home's holiness, but too often Christians have forgotten. We relegate God to our churches, forgetting that most of Christ's ministry, including the Last Supper, took place in private homes.

Just as in those days, our homes are meant to be welcoming places, places of security and grace that reflect God's nature. [2]

❧

How would my family's attitude about housework change if we thought of our home as God's, a place where we have asked Him to dwell?

A Mother's Heart

The house is old, the trees are bare,
    Moonless above bends twilight's dome;
But what on earth is half so dear,
    So longed for, as the hearth of home?
                                    —*Emily Brontë*

∽

Dear Lord, thank You for my home. I ask that You fill it with Your Holy Spirit. Even when I don't have time to polish and dust, may it still shine with Your welcome and love, so that whoever comes in my doors senses that You are present.

Please help me, God, not to fill my home with irritation and frustration; help me not to think that because I'm in the privacy of my own home, I can indulge in "house-sin." Instead, may my husband and my children and I hand grace back and forth to each other. Amen.

THE FRUSTRATIONS
OF DAILY LIFE

" 'Martha, Martha, thou art careful and troubled about many things: But one thing is needful: and Mary hath chosen that good part, which shall not be taken away from her.' "

—*Luke 10:41–42*

∾

Despite our best intentions, all of us have times when life presses down on us so hard that we yield to frustration and anger. Frustration can spring from something as little as a toddler's spilled bowl of Cheerios across our freshly swept kitchen floor—or an adolescent's rebellion may make frustration grip our throat. We work so hard; after all that we do, when our efforts seem to come to nothing, we too feel like rebelling.

REBELLION

Rebellion can be healthy, for rebellion is the thing that says, "It's not fair!" It's what makes us stand up for our rights against forces that would squash us. It's what makes us fight for change.

But much of our rebellion rises from our need to be at the center. When we whine, "It's not fair," a lot of the time we really mean we should have not only our equal share, but the biggest and the best. "I *should* be at the center of the world. It's not fair that they won't let me."

When our rebellion clashes with our children's, then as disciplinarians we are no longer successful. Instead we ride a teeter-totter between, "They are bad children," and "I am a bad mother." If our children's behavior makes them "bad," then we are entitled to our anger, our need to control their behavior. But our feelings of aggression against our children make most of us uneasy and then down we go into depression and guilt. . . . Whether we're up or down on this teeter-totter, we are in no position to discipline our children with authority.

Authority is a word many of us don't like. Our society is no longer at the far end of the pendulum swing, as it was in the sixties, when experts recommended absolute permissiveness to parents as they raised children. Still, we've all been influenced by the ideals of freedom and democracy, and we certainly don't want to return to the days when children were to be seen and not heard. . . .

Christ's perspective on authority was different from ours, though. Let the person " 'who is the greatest among you must become like the youngest,' " he said, " 'and the leader like the servant' " (Luke 22:26 NAS). In other words, authority is not hierarchical, and our authority as parents does not come from the fact that we are stronger and our children weaker. Instead, Jesus put authority in the same realm with service and humility. " 'Now that I, your Lord and Teacher, have washed your feet, you also should wash one another's feet' " (John 13:14 NIV). Our authority as mothers springs from our willingness to serve our children in the most ordinary and menial ways.

This concept of authority has less to do with control than it does with love, with teaching a way of life through action. When, as mothers, we follow Christ's example, we are less likely to find our rebellion bumping heads with our children's, for we cannot teach what is not true for ourselves. We can only discipline our children in ways we ourselves experience as real.

As women, though, sometimes we're tired of always being the selfless, giving ones. Sometimes we want to throw a tantrum and be as selfish as our two-year-olds. *We* have our rights, after all, and we're tired of lying on the floor while the entire family wipes their feet on us. We long for freedom. We're sick of being sweet.

John Wesley, the eighteenth-century theologian who founded Methodism, recommended that we allow discipline to build in our natures "humility,

meekness, yieldingness, gentleness, sweetness."
These sound like feminine qualities. . .but Wesley's
system of discipline, his "Methods of Holiness,"
was not written for women so much as men. He
advocated that all people follow holy lifestyles so
that the inner person would be molded into Christ's
image. Maybe we women have tended to already
demonstrate these qualities because down through
the years we have been disciplined by motherhood's
methods. . . .

Our obedience to the limitations of our lives, our
love and commitment to our children, is the thing
that makes us not only able to discipline ourselves
but our children too. If we follow our rebellion, then
we will knock down the walls of our own house. . . .

Too often rebellion makes us pursue an illusion, a
make-believe freedom that gets in the way of our real
freedom. Our need to be at the center of the world will
only enslave us to our egos. This slavery is sterile and
nonproductive. Just as when we follow a recipe,
write a poem, do carpentry, or sew a quilt, creativity
requires that we work within a framework of rules.
Motherhood is like a tree that needs commitment's
deep roots—and tethered by these roots we grow. [1]

∽

> Stone walls do not a prison make
>   Nor iron bars a cage;
> Minds innocent and quiet take
>   That for an hermitage;
> If I have freedom in my love,

And in my soul am free;
Angels alone, that soar above,
Enjoy such liberty.

—*Richard Lovelace*

❧

"Every wise woman buildeth her house:
but the foolish plucketh it down with her hands."
—*Proverbs 14:1*

❧

Because I was impatient, would not wait,
And thrust my willful hand across Thy threads,
And marred the pattern drawn out for my life,
O Lord, I do repent.

—*Sarah Williams*

❧

In the selection that follows, Martin Luther suggests that the reason we often feel so frustrated is that we are looking for "the peace the world gives." In other words, we are looking for the peace that comes when everything goes the way we want. God's peace, however, is different from the world's; even when everything looks like it is going wrong, we can find the peace of Christ alive in our hearts.

TRUE PEACE OF MIND

You do indeed "seek peace and ensue it," but altogether in the wrong way. You seek the peace the world gives, not the peace Christ gives.

Are you not aware how God is so wonderful among His people that He has set His peace where there is no peace, that is in the midst of all our trials? As He says, "Rule thou in the midst of thine enemies."

It is not, therefore, that person whom no one bothers who has peace. That kind of peace is the peace the world gives. It is the person who everyone disturbs and everyone harasses, and yet, who joyfully and quietly endures them all.

You are saying with Israel, "Peace! Peace!" when there is no peace. Say, rather with Christ, "Cross! Cross!"—and there is no cross. For the cross ceases to be a cross the moment you say gladly, "Blessed cross! Of all the trees that are in the wood there is none such as thee!"

Seek this peace and you will find peace. Seek for nothing else than to take on trials with joy. . . . You will never find this peace by seeking and choosing what you feel and judge to be the path of peace.

—*Martin Luther*

∽

[She] who cannot forgive others breaks the bridge over which [she] must pass [herself].

—*George Herbert*

∽

"A soft answer turneth away wrath."

—*Proverbs 15:1*

Maybe the secret to finding God's joy even in the midst of frustration is to simply say "yes" to whatever He sends into our life—even that bowl of spilled Cheerios!

Sometimes, though, the people we live with are the biggest frustrations of all. In the story that follows, Katy finds this to be true when her husband's sister comes to live with them.

FRUSTRATIONS WITH IN-LAWS

The butter was horrible. Martha had insisted that she alone was capable of selecting that article and had ordered a quantity from her own village that I could not eat myself and was ashamed to have on my table. I pushed back my plate in disgust.

"I hope, Martha, that you have not ordered much of this odious stuff!" I cried.

Martha replied that it was of the very first quality and appealed to her father and Ernest, who both agreed with her, which I thought was very unkind and unjust. I rushed into a hot debate on the subject, during which Ernest maintained that ominous silence that indicates his not being pleased, and that irritated me and led me on. . . .

Here Ernest put in a little oil.

"I think you are both right," he said. ". . .This can be used for making seedcakes and we can get a new supply."

This was his masterpiece! A whole firkin of

butter made up into seedcakes!

Martha turned to encounter him on that head, and I slipped off to my room to look, with a miserable sense of disappointment, at my folly and weakness in making so much ado about nothing. I find it hard to believe that it can do me good to have people live with me who like rancid butter and who disagree with me in everything else.

In desperation, Katy seeks advice from a wise older friend.

"You know," I began, "dear Mrs. Campbell, that there are some trials that cannot do us good. They only call out all there is in us that is unlovely and severe."

"I don't know of any such trials," she replied.

"Suppose you had to live with people who were perfectly uncongenial, who misunderstood you, and who were always getting into your way as stumbling blocks?"

"If I were living with them and they made me unhappy, I would ask God to relieve me of this trial if He thought it best. If He did not think it best, I would then try to find out the reason. He might have two reasons. One would be the good they might do me. The other, the good I might do them."

"But in the case I was supposing, neither party can be of the least use to the other."

"You forget perhaps the indirect good one may gain by living with uncongenial, tempting persons.

First, such people do good by the very self-denial and self-control their mere presence demands. Then, their making one's home less homelike and perfect than it would be in their absence may help to render our real home in heaven more attractive."

"But suppose one cannot exercise self-control and is always flying out and flaring up?" I objected.

"I should say that a Christian who was always doing that," she replied, gravely, "was in pressing need of just the trial God sent when He shut that person up to such a life of hourly temptation. We only know ourselves what we really are when the force of circumstances brings us out."

"It is very mortifying and painful to find how weak one is."

"That is true. But our mortifications are some of God's best physicians and do much toward healing our pride and self-conceit."

"Do you really think, then, that God deliberately appoints to some of His children a lot where their worst passions are excited, with a desire to bring good out of this seemingly evil? Why, I have always supposed the best thing that could happen to me, for instance, would be to have a home exactly to my mind; a home where all were forebearing, loving, and good-tempered, a sort of little heaven below."

"If you have not such a home, my dear, are you sure it is not partly your own fault?"

"Of course it is my own fault. Because I am very quick-tempered, I want to live with good-tempered people."

"That is very benevolent in you," she said archly. I colored but went on.

"Oh, I know I am selfish. And therefore I want to live with those who are not so. I want to live with persons to whom I can look for an example and who will constantly stimulate me to something higher."

"But if God chooses quite another lot for you, you may be sure that He sees that you need something totally different from what you want. You said just now that you would gladly go through any trial in order to attain a personal love for Christ that should become the ruling principle of your life. Now as soon as God sees this desire in you, is He not kind, is He not wise in appointing such trials as He knows will lead to this end?" [2]

∽

The question is not what a [woman] can scorn, or disparage, or find fault with, but what [she] can love, and value, and appreciate.

—*John Ruskin*

∽

Like Katy in Stepping Heavenward, *all of us have times when we long to be spiritual women— and yet other people seem to get in our way. We truly love our families, and most of the time we serve them with joy. But sometimes all the many responsibilities that come with caring for a family may seem like too much. We'd like to run away and have lunch with a friend, read a book, go for a walk, wander around the mall—anything except do another load of laundry, vacuum another floor, or cook another meal. In* The Christian's Secret of a Happy Life, *Hannah Whitehall Smith expressed these same frustrations. . .*

WHEN SERVICE TO OTHERS SEEMS A HEAVY BURDEN

Have you never gone to work as a slave to his daily task, believing it to be your duty and that therefore you must do it, but rebounding like an Indian-rubber ball back into your real interests and pleasures the moment your work was over?

You have known of course that this was the wrong way to feel, and have been thoroughly ashamed of it, but still you have seen no way to help it. You have not *loved* your work; and, could you have done so with an easy conscience, you would have been glad to give it up all together. . . .

It is altogether the way we look at things, whether we think they are crosses or not. . . . What we need in the Christian life is to. . .*want* to do God's will as much as other people want to do their own will. And this is the idea of the Gospel. It is what God intended for us; and it is what He promised. In describing the new covenant in Hebrews 8:6–13, He says it shall no more be the old covenant made on Sinai—that is, a law given from the outside, controlling a man by force—but it shall be a law written *within,* constraining us by love.

"I will put my laws," He says, "into their mind, and write them in their hearts." . . .Nothing could possibly be conceived more effectual than this. How often have we thought when dealing with our children, "Oh, if I could only get inside them, and make them *want* to do just what I want, how easy it would be to manage them!" How often in practical experience we have found that to deal with cross-grained people we must carefully avoid suggesting our wishes to them, but must in some way induce them to suggest the thing themselves. . . . And we, who are by nature a stiff-necked people, always rebel more or less against a law from outside of us, while we joyfully embrace the same law springing up within.

God's way of working, therefore, is to get possession of the inside of us, to take the control and management of our will, and to work it for us. The obedience is easy and a delight, and service becomes freedom, until the Christian is forced to explain, "This happy service! Who could dream earth had such liberty?"

What you need to do, then, dear Christian, if you are in bondage in the matter of service, is to put your will over completely into the hands of your Lord, surrendering to Him the entire control of it. Say, "Yes, Lord, YES!" to everything, and trust Him to work in you so as to bring your whole wishes and affections into conformity with His own sweet, and lovable, and most lovely will. . . .

In this way of life, no burdens are carried, no

anxieties felt. The Lord is our burden-bearer, and upon Him we must lay off every care. He says, in effect, "Be careful for nothing, but make your requests known to me, and I will attend them all."

Be careful for *nothing,* He says, not even your service. Why? Because we are so utterly helpless that no matter how *careful* we were, our service would amount to nothing! . . . In truth, if we only knew it, our chief fitness for service is in our utter helplessness. His strength is made perfect, not in our strength, but in our weakness. Our strength is only a hindrance.[3]

∽

How good to know that when we are the weakest, that God has room in our lives to be strong. We tend to think we should give God our strengths—the things we do well, the days when we accomplish a lot, the moments when we feel pride in our own abilities. Of course we should give God these; but even more, we should give Him our weaknesses— the things we're not good at, the days when we can't seem to get anything done at all, our embarrassment when we fail. When we can humbly offer everything up to God, then we will have learned Hannah Whitall Smith's secret of a happy life.

∽

"But the fruit of the Spirit is love, joy, peace, longsuffering, gentleness, goodness, faith, meekness, temperance."

—*Galatians 5:22–23*

Dear Father, help me to give You everything today: the things I do well—and the things at which I fail. Empower me to say "yes" to everything, even life's daily frustrations. Thank You that when I am weak, You are strong. Amen.

BECOMING COMFORTABLE WITH OURSELVES

Grow old along with me!
The best is yet to be,
The last of life, for which the first was made.
Our times are in His hand.

—*Robert Browning*

∽

"Favour is deceitful, and beauty is vain:
but a woman that feareth the LORD,
she shall be praised."

—*Proverbs 31:30*

∽

Our society fears old age. As women who belong to Christ, though, we have nothing to fear from growing older. Instead, we can look forward to learning more about ourselves in relation to God— and as we do, we will find we are more and more comfortable being simply ourselves, the women God created.

In the following selection, a grown son speaks with his mother, explaining how his war experiences helped him to understand that even our pain and flaws can be used by God. In fact, they can be the very points where we touch grace. This is a vital lesson that only age and experience can bring.

CONSECRATING OUR PAIN AND OUR FAULTS

"In the war I disliked the aftereffects of wounds and gas intensely," said Hilary. "When you are burned, and can't get your breath, and are afraid you are going blind, it is impossible to pray. And then one day, with great difficulty, I suddenly put into practice and knew as truth what of course I had always known theoretically, that if pain is offered to God as prayer the pain and prayer are synonymous. A sort of substitution takes place that is like the old story of 'Beauty and the Beast.' The utterly abominable Thing that prevents your prayer becomes your prayer. And you know what prayer is, Mother. It's all of a piece, the prayer of a mystic or a child, adoration or intercession, it's all the same thing; whether you feel it or not it is union with God. . . . Once you have managed the wrenching effort of substitution the abominable Thing, while remaining utterly detestable for yourself, becomes the channel of grace for others and so the dearest treasure that you have. And if it happens to be a secret treasure that you need not speak about to another, then that's all the better. Somehow the secrecy increases its value."

"You put it better than I could do," said Lucilla gently. "I did feel after that way of prayer in the war, but I did not try hard enough, and when the war was over I fell away. But I recognize what you say as a truth that I know."

"Of course," said Hilary, "I do not think that anyone who has experienced disaster is not in some way aware of one of the fundamental paradoxes of our existence. Only we don't live in a perpetual state of disaster, and it doesn't occur to us to apply the paradox to the worries and frustrations and irritations among which we do perpetually live. We lack the humility."

"Well, really," said Lucilla, "if I couldn't put up with my everyday worries and aches and pains without having to regard them as prayer I should feel myself a poor sort of coward."

"As I said," remarked Hilary dryly, "we lack the humility. One feels ridiculous, as you don't feel ridiculous when it is some disaster. But it's not just the way you look at it, it's a deliberate and costly action of the will. It can be a real wrenching of the soul. Yet the more you practice it, the fresher and greener grows your life. And it's the same with joys as with disaster and the Things that annoy us, lifted up with the same hard effort, even the earthly joys are points of contact and have the freshness of eternity in them."

"It's like plants," Lucilla said. "The thrust upwards means a corresponding growth of root down. Sun and water. I believe I am beginning to learn to accept myself, Hilary, but I see now that acceptance is only the first step. If I can't stop worrying (and anguish for the children is part of motherhood, Hilary, one can't get rid of it) at least I'll worry in a different way." [1]

∽

Women are never stronger than when they arm
themselves with their weaknesses.
—*Madame du Deffand*

∽

We grow old as soon as we cease to love and trust.
—*Madame de Choiseul*

∽

When a woman ceases to alter the fashion
of her hair, you guess that she has passed
the crisis of her experience.
—*Mary Austin*

∽

I do not ask for any crown
But that which all may win;
Nor try to conquer any world
Except the one within.
—*Louisa May Alcott*

Youth tends to be full of pride. As we mature, however, with God's help, we learn to accept even our failures. Julian of Norwich, a woman who lived in England six hundred years ago, speaks of this acceptance in the light of God's mercy.

Accepting Our Failures

And when we have fallen, through frailty or blindness, then our courteous Lord touches us, stirs and calls us. And then He wills that we should see our wretchedness and humbly acknowledge it. But it is not His will that we should stay like this, nor does He will that we should busy ourselves too much with self-accusations; nor is it His will that we should despise ourselves. But He wills that we should quickly turn to Him.

He is quick to clasp us to Himself, for we are His joy and His delight, and He is our salvation and our life.

Wonderful and splendid is the place where the Lord lives. And therefore it is His will that we turn quickly at His gracious touch, rejoicing more in the fullness of His love than sorrowing over our frequent failures.

—*Julian of Norwich*

Women wish to be loved without a why or a wherefore; not because they are pretty or good, or well-bred, or graceful, or intelligent, but because they are themselves.

—*Henri-Frederic Amiel*

∽

We try to be gentle with others—but often we forget to be gentle with ourselves. True humility, however, means not thinking too much about ourselves—not even about our faults and failures. Instead, our concentration should be on Christ and His grace. This sort of consecrated humility helps us as we mature to become more comfortable "inside our own skin."

GENTLENESS TO OURSELVES

One form of gentleness we should practice is towards ourselves. We should never get irritable with ourselves because of our imperfections. It is reasonable to be displeased and sorry when we commit faults, but not fretful or spiteful to ourselves.

Some make the mistake of being angry because they have been angry, hurt because they have been hurt, vexed because they have been vexed. They think they are getting rid of anger, that the second remedies the first; actually, they are preparing the way for fresh anger on the first occasion.

Besides this, all irritation with ourselves tends to foster pride and springs from self-love, which is displeased at finding we are not perfect.

We should regard our faults with calm, collected and firm displeasure. We correct them better by a quiet persevering repentance than by an irritated, hasty, and passionate one.

When your heart has fallen, raise it gently, humbling yourself before God, acknowledging your fault, but not surprised at your fall.

—*Francis de Sales*

∽

Hide not your talents, they for use were made,
What's a Sun-Dial in the Shade?
—*Benjamin Franklin*

∽

One way to become more comfortable with ourselves is by accepting our daily routines. Sometimes we dream of other women's lives, lives of greater glamour or prestige. God may call some of us to follow our dreams—but in the meantime, as Teresa of Avila says, we must be "willing and ready to do what our Lord asks us"—even housework. We don't like to think of ourselves as servants—but our self-concepts may change when we realize that all of us, no matter what we do, can be servants of the King.

BE CONTENT TO BE A MARTHA

His Majesty does not lead all souls by the same way. . . . Would you not be content to resemble the blessed woman who received Christ our Lord so often into her home, where she fed and served Him, and where He ate at her table?

Imagine that your home's little community is the house of Martha where there must be different kinds of people. Remember that someone must cook the meals and count yourselves happy in being able to serve like Martha.

Reflect that true humility consists in being willing and ready to do what our Lord asks of us. . . . Then if contemplation, prayer, nursing the sick, the work of the house, and the most menial labor, all serve this Guest, why should we choose to minister to Him in one way rather than in another?

—Teresa of Avila

∽

You will find, as you look back upon your life, that the moments when you have really lived are the moments when you have done things in the spirit of love.

—Henry Drummond

∽

The heart has its own memory like the mind, And in it are enshrined the precious keepsakes, into which is wrought the giver's loving thought.

—Henry Wadsworth Longfellow

∽

Katy in Stepping Heavenward *discovers the same*

lesson of which Teresa of Avila wrote hundreds of years earlier. As mothers we do not have to fear that we are missing out on "real life." Instead, God meets us here, in our day-to-day responsibilities to our families. When we can accept our lives as the gifts that they are from God, then we will find ourselves comfortable with who we are, delighting in the unique ways God speaks to us.

THE VOCATION OF MATERNITY

"The best convent," I said, "for a woman is the seclusion of her own home. There she may find her vocation and fight her battles, and there she may learn the reality and the earnestness of life."

"Pshaw!" cried she. "Excuse me, however, for saying that; but some of the most brilliant girls I know have settled down into mere married women and spend their whole time nursing babies! Think how belittling!"

"Is it more so than spending it dressing, driving, dancing, and the like?"

"Of course it is. I had a friend once who shone like a star in society. She married and had four children as fast as she could. Well! What was the consequence? She lost her beauty, her spirit and animation, lost her youth, and lost her health. The only earthly things she can talk about are teething, dieting, and measles!"

I laughed at this exaggeration. . . . "As you have spoken plainly to me, knowing me to be a wife and mother, you must allow me to speak plainly in return," I began. ". . . You will permit me to say that when you speak contemptuously of the vocation of maternity, you dishonor not only the mother who bore you but the Lord Jesus Himself, who chose to be born of woman and to be ministered unto by her through a helpless infancy. . . ."

I thought of my dear ones. . . and I thought of my love for them and theirs for me. And I thought of Him who alone gives reality to even such joys as these. [2]

∽

"He maketh the barren woman to keep house,
and to be a joyful mother of children.
Praise ye the LORD."
—*Psalm 113:9*

∽

In spite of illness one can remain alive past the usual date of disintegration if one is unafraid of change, insatiable in intellectual curiosity, interested in big things, and happy in small ways.
—*Edith Wharton*

∽

Beauty—be not caused—It is—
Chase it, and it ceases—
Chase it not, and it abides.
—*Emily Dickinson*

To love abundantly is to live abundantly,
and to love forever is to live forever.

—*Anonymous*

∽

*Being a beautiful woman, a fulfilled woman, are
not goals we can chase and grab. Instead, our beauty
and fulfillment are side effects that spring from our
commitment to Christ. As we live His abundant life,
interested in His world and delighting ourselves in all
the tiny blessings He sends our way, we will find that
we are beautiful and fulfilled simply because we are
God's. Growing old in God's presence will only bring
still more beauty and fulfillment.*

*The following selection describes the old age
of someone who experienced this, a seventeenth-
century man named Brother Lawrence.*

One Who Has Grown Old in God's Presence

You should know that during the more than forty
years he has been in religion, he has concentrated
continually on being always with God, doing nothing, saying nothing, and thinking nothing which
might displease Him. He does this for no other reason except love of God. . . .

If sometimes he strays a little from the divine
presence, God soon touches him to remind him,
often even when he is the busiest with his work. He

answers these reminders faithfully, either by lifting up his heart to God, by gazing lovingly at Him, or by speaking words of love (for example, *My God, here I am, all Yours; Lord, shape me like Your heart*). And then it seems to him (in fact, he feels it) that this God of love, satisfied with these few words, returns and rests in the very deep center of his soul. . . .

You can guess from this what contentment and satisfaction he enjoys, continually finding in himself so great a treasure. He is no longer searching for it anxiously; he has it always open before him and may help himself whenever he wants. . . .

Let us make way for grace; let us make for the time we have lost, since we may have little time left. Death is close behind us; let's be ready for it. . . .

Again I say, let's search ourselves. Time presses down on us. . . . But those who have the Holy Spirit's breeze blowing on them move forward even while they're sleeping. If our soul's ship is battered and tossed by wind and storm, then let us wake up the Lord who is resting in our hearts. He will soon calm the sea. [3]

∽

Beauty seen is never lost.
—*John Greenleaf Whittier*

∽

We are shaped and fashioned by what we love.
—*Johann Wolfgang von Goethe*

An archeologist is the best husband any woman can have: the older she gets, the more interested he is in her.

—*Agatha Christie*

It is better to be faithful than famous.
—*Theodore Roosevelt*

Though we travel the world over to find the beautiful, we must carry it with us, or we find it not.
—*Ralph Waldo Emerson*

We will never wake up one day and find that we have "arrived" at perfect maturity. As Martin Luther wrote so long ago, we are all still in the process of becoming the people God wants us to be. Let's adapt the common saying and apply it to ourselves: Be patient with yourself—God's not finished with you yet!

Daily Life:
A Pilgrimage to Heaven

This life is not a state of being righteous, but rather a growth of righteousness; not a state of being healthy, but a period of healing; not a state of being, but becoming; not a state of rest, but of exercise and activity.

A MOTHER'S HEART

We are not yet what we shall be,
    but we grow toward it;
The process is not yet finished,
    but is still going on;
This life is not the end,
    it is the way to a better.
All does not yet shine with glory;
    nevertheless, all is being purified.
                                    —*Martin Luther*

∽

"The king's daughter is all glorious within."
                                    —*Psalm 45:13*

∽

Thank You, Jesus, that my beauty comes from You. Help me not to worry about the world's standards. Remind me that You do not expect me to look like a Barbie doll. As I grow older, may I become more and more comfortable with who I am, the woman You created in Your image. Amen.

WORRIES

No coward soul is mine,
No trembler in the world's storm-troubled
    sphere:
I see Heaven's glories shine,
And faith shines equal, arming me from
    fear.

—Emily Brontë

～

*Worrying just seems to come with motherhood's
territory. It's a bad habit we all fall into. As Emily
Brontë's poem says, the only solution is to keep our
eyes fixed on "Heaven's glories" rather than the
"world's storm-troubled sphere." Faith is our only
shield against fear and worry.*

SEPARATION ANXIETY

Sometimes we find we can trust God for our own
lives more easily than we can for our children's. To

watch our children's gradual separation from our protection and care radically tests our faith in God's reality. But if we truly believe that God's grace is real and active, then we must believe it is equally real and equally active in our children's lives. . . .

Worrying comes easily to mothers, though. It's hard to let go, but the most often repeated commandment in the Bible is "Fear not!" Fear makes us cling. It weighs us down and it slows our progress on motherhood's spiritual path.

Faith lets go. [1]

∞

She never quite leaves her children at home,
   even when she doesn't take them along.
                    —*Margaret Culkin Banning*

∞

Sometimes we feel weighted down with the burden of seeing to our children's health and safety. The world is full of dangers that threaten our children's lives—and we yield to the false thinking that says only we, their mothers, can keep them safe. We know that our children's needs must come first, and so we feel we must give up every other ministry or profession, and devote ourselves totally to their well-being.

We forget that both we and our children are in God's hands. We can never protect our children from every danger, for only God can truly see to their well-being—and when we put ourselves in His hands, He can balance our motherhood with our other occupations. The following episode from the life of a missionary mother shows how God can provide for both ourselves and our children when we are entirely committed to Him.

THE STORY OF ONE FURLOUGH

"And call upon me in the day of trouble:
I will deliver thee, and thou shalt glorify me."
—*Psalm 50:15*

∽

In the summer of 1908 I was obliged to return to Canada with five of our children, leaving Mr. Goforth in China for the revival work.

Reaching Toronto, I learned that my eldest son was at death's door from repeated attacks of rheumatic fever. He was then still almost a day's journey away. On my way there, as I recalled the times in which he had been given back to us from the very gates of death, my faith was strengthened to believe for his recovery again. But, as I prayed, it became clear that the answers to my petition depended on myself; in other words, that I must yield myself and my will to God.

I had been planning to take no meetings during that furlough, but to devote myself wholly to my children. I now confessed the sin of planning my own life, and definitely covenanted with the Lord that if He would raise my son for His service, I would take meetings or do anything, as He opened the way for the care of the children.

There were six difficult doors, however, that would have to be opened—not one, but all—before I could possibly go out and speak for Christ and China, as God seemed to be asking. First, the Lord would need to restore my son to complete health, as I could never feel justified in leaving a sick child. Second, He would need to restore my own health, for I had been ordered to the hospital for an operation. Third, He would need to keep all the other children well. Fourth, a servant must be sent to take care of the house—though my income was so small that a servant seemed out of the question, and only the strictest economy was making both ends meet. Fifth, a Christian lady would need to be willing to take care of the children, and act as my housekeeper in my absences from home. Sixth, sufficient money would need to be sent to meet the extra expenses incurred by my leaving home.

Yet, as I laid these difficulties before the Lord, I received the definite assurance that He would open the way.

My son was brought back to Toronto on a stretcher, the doctor not allowing him to raise his head; but on arrival, he would not obey orders, declaring that he was so well he could not and would not remain still. Fearing the consequences of his disobeying orders, I telephoned for the doctor to come at once. On his arrival he gave the lad a thorough examination, and then said: "Well, I cannot make him out; all I can say is, let him do as he pleases."

Within a month the boy was going to his high school, apparently quite well. Some months later he applied for a position as forester under the government. He had to pass through the hands of the official doctor. My son told him of his recent illness, and of what the doctor had said concerning his heart, but this physician replied: "I can discover nothing whatever the matter with you, and will therefore give you a clear bill of health."

As for myself, I did not go to the hospital; for all the symptoms that had seemed to require it left me, and I became perfectly well. A servant was sent to me who did her work sympathetically, as helping me to do the Lord's work. A married niece, living near, offered to stay in my home whenever I needed to be absent.

And so there remained but one condition unfulfilled—the money. But I believed this would come as I went forward; and it did.

Under these circumstances I dared not refuse invitations to speak. Yet, so weak was my faith, for months I never left home for a few days without dreading lest something should happen to the children during my absence. I even accepted meetings with the proviso that if the children needed me I must fail to keep my appointment. But as the days and weeks and months passed, and all went well, I learned to trust.

"Be still; be strong today."
But, Lord, tomorrow?
What of tomorrow, Lord?
Shall there be rest from toil,
Be truce from sorrow?
"Did I not die for thee?
Do I not live for thee?
Leave Me tomorrow."

I wish to make clear that, had I been living a life of ease or self-indulgence, I could not have been justified in expecting God to undertake for me in such matters as are here recorded. It must be remembered that I had stepped out into a life which meant *trusting for everything*.

Before leaving China for Canada my husband had said to me: "Do not stint the children with apples; give them all they want." But when I began housekeeping I found this was not very easy to do. Apples were expensive, and the appetites of my six children for them seemed insatiable. However, I began by buying a few small baskets; and then I did not need to buy more, for apples came in a most wonderful way. First in baskets; then, as the season advanced, in barrels.

I feel that the Lord saw that I had given up all for Him, so just showed how He could provide, thus evidencing His love and care for my dear children. We had set up housekeeping at the end of the fruit season, and so I had not been able to do canning for winter use. That winter, again and again, gifts of canned fruit came, sometimes from unknown sources. Altogether, seventy jars of the finest fruit were sent to us.

However, shortly before leaving home for ten days, the servant informed me that the canned fruit was finished. Accordingly, I went down and ordered enough dry fruit to last until I should return. On reaching home I was greeted at the door by a rush of children, all trying at once to tell me that a lovely valentine had just arrived. Leading me back to the kitchen, they showed me the table covered with twenty jars of the most delicious-looking fruit, and a large can of maple syrup. On a card accompanying the gift was written, "A valentine." [2]

∽

"When it snows, she has no fear for her household; for all of them are clothed in scarlet"
—Proverbs 31:21 (NIV)

∽

God not only provided for the Goforth family's basic needs—He also provided that extra treat: a large can of maple syrup. When we trust God, He will care for all the ordinary day-to-day things our children need—and He will also see that they have those special sweet extras. Just as the proverb says, our children will not only be clothed—they will be clothed in scarlet! But first, we must leave them in His hands.

"And all thy children shall be taught of the LORD;
and great shall be the peace of thy children."
—*Isaiah 54:13*

∽

Thank You, Father, for being not only my Father but my children's. When I am scared and worried for their safety and well-being, help me to trust them each to You, knowing that You love them far more than I am capable. Thank You that You will always watch them, even when I cannot. I know they can never go so far from home that they will be lost to Your love. Please, dear Father, give them their daily bread—and now and then, feed them apples and maple syrup too! When it snows, I know You will see that they are clothed in scarlet. Amen.

STRENGTH IN ADVERSITY

We never know how high we are
    Till we are called to rise;
And then, if we are true to plan,
    Our statures touch the skies.
                —Emily Dickinson

~

Hard times come sooner or later to us all. When they do, we find out just what Christ's salvation means, in real and practical ways. Even in the midst of trouble, though, He will, as Emily Dickinson said, help us "touch the skies."

SAFE AM I

Evangelical Christians use the word *saved* a lot. It's one of those terms we've said and heard so often that we don't even stop to think about what the word means. Much of the time, we use it to categorize the people around us: so-and-so is saved, so-and-so isn't.

In other words, *saved* has become synonymous with *Christian,* a follower of Christ. And of course, the followers of Christ *are* saved. But what does that mean?

Webster says that to save means "to rescue or deliver from danger or harm," or "to preserve or guard from injury, destruction, or loss." As a child growing up in Sunday school, those were the two meanings I used to think of when I heard talk of Jesus saving: First, I'd picture Christ rescuing me from some terrible danger, throwing me a lifesaver when I was drowning, carrying me in His arms from a burning house; and then I'd picture Him keeping me, treasuring me, the same way I like to "save" all sorts of things on the shelves in my bedroom.

You see, I've always hated to throw things away. When I was a kid, I had a collection of apparently useless objects: colored pens that didn't work, my cat's old flea collars, bits of ribbon and wrinkled wrapping paper; in my sight they were all precious and I saved them carefully. Today the things I save are different (old letters, my children's drawings), but the principle is the same: I hate to let go of things, I hate to throw them away into oblivion.

But before I had children I never worried about people getting tossed away, forgotten, and I certainly never worried about my own permanence. Death held no terrors for me back then. In fact, I prided myself on my faith, my utter confidence that, just as Jesus had promised, my life would never end.

And then a series of miscarriages changed everything. I finally understood that my smug, fearless faith wasn't faith at all. Instead it was the self-centered arrogance of youth, an egotistical confidence in my own self rather than Christ's saving grace. For the first time I realized that death was a reality that I and my loved ones would have to pass through; we had no hope of escape, and I was overwhelmed with fear. What if death meant that me and my family—all our hopes and memories, all our love, our dislikes and little pleasures and ideas, all that makes us who we are—would be discarded like crumpled letters or smudged drawings, dropped into oblivion?

I wasn't afraid of hell, but nothingness. I could not bear to think that someday we might all simply cease to be. The thought was a constant nightmare lurking at the edges of my thoughts. Maybe that's why Paul speaks of putting on the "hope of salvation as a helmet" (1 Thessalonians 5:8 NIV), because he knew that hope will protect our heads, our minds, from the nightmare fears that come with grief and loss. I had foolishly removed my helmet, leaving myself vulnerable to attack.

But like a lifesaver being tossed into dark, stormy water, like strong arms carrying me through black, billowing smoke, in the midst of my pain and turmoil I heard that old familiar word whispered: "saved, saved, saved." Gradually, that worn word I had taken for granted for years began to gleam in the midst of my darkness. I understood anew that Christ truly is my Savior, for He redeems my life from destruction (Psalm 103:4), He delivers, and He rescues (Daniel 6:27). As long as I and my family put our faith in Christ, we will never be thrown away; instead, we will be "preserved blameless unto the coming of our Lord Jesus Christ" (1 Thessalonians 5:23). We are truly saved. [1]

∽

No matter what adversity comes to us in life, Christ is the lifesaver who will help us float through life's storms, alive and well despite the dark skies and crashing waves.

∽

Necessity can set me helpless on my back,
   but she cannot keep me there;
nor can four walls limit my vision.
                    —*Margaret Fairless Barber*

∽

Jesus, I ask for Your help when hard times knock me down. Remind me that through Your strength, I can always get back to my feet. Thank You that You have saved me for eternity. Amen.

OUR HEAVENLY
COMPANION

Be thou my Vision,
    O Lord of my heart;
Nought be all else to me,
    Save that Thou art.

                        —*Mary Byrne*

∽

Through all of motherhood's joys and sorrows, fulfillment and frustration, we have a Companion who never leaves us, whether we sense His presence or not. He smiles and laughs with us; He cries with us and understands our frustrations. In every aspect of a mother's heart, we find images of this holy Companion. He never leaves us.

GOD WITH US

My mind and my heart gradually became so joined to God that He was continually with me in everything.

The more my love grew, the more I became aware of my own sins and my dependence upon God.

Lying in my bed I heard the Lord call my name. I listened in silence until He spoke. "Where God is, heaven is. God is in your soul night and day. When you go to church I go with you; when you sit down for a meal I sit with you; when you lie down to sleep I lie with you and when you go out I go with you."

—*Margery Kempe*

∾

All the way my Saviour leads me;
　　What have I to ask beside?
Can I doubt His tender mercy,
　　Who through life has been my Guide?

—*Fanny Crosby*

∾

We've all heard the story of the footprints in the sand: A person and God had walked hand in hand, leaving two sets of prints behind. But in some places one set of prints disappeared, leaving the other's all alone. "Why did You leave me to walk all alone?" the person asked God. And God replied, "Those are not your footprints you see but Mine, for those are the places where I carried you."

The following excerpt tells of a woman who has just lost a child to death. Exhausted from grief, she falls asleep and dreams of a bird who has accompanied her with song throughout her life, even when she failed to hear.

A GLIMPSE OF HEAVEN

As she slept she dreamed one of those astonishingly vivid dreams that make the dreamer feel that his soul has actually left his body and gone voyaging. She was walking through a forest in a strange country. About her the great trees soared upwards, stretching their branches against the sky like arms held up in adoration. They were like living creatures, those trees, and so were the myriad flowers that grew about her feet. In their color and scent they were as an army that praised God; the ground was singing—bright with them. There were caroling birds in the trees who did not fly away when she came near them, and little brown furry beasts in the undergrowth who had never known the meaning of fear. There was water not far away. She could hear the murmur of it and see the calm blue of it shining through the trees. And yet behind this music there was a deep quiet. The music and the silence, the movement and the rest seemed coexistent together. She felt happy with a quite indescribable happiness that was yet best described by the word cleanliness. In body, mind, and spirit she felt clean, with her thoughts unmuddied and her body a perfect instrument of the spirit within her that she could feel was a polished mirror to reflect and transmit the light about her.

That light too was indescribable. It was something like the light of earthly dawn, holding the same depth of color, the same coolness and warmth as the light of the sun and moon shining together; yet it transcended that as greatly as the light of the sun transcends the flicker of the candle. The music that was all about her, lovely yet diffuse as light, seemed to gather itself into one single phrase, as when the voice of a solo singer soars out above the harmony of orchestra and voices, and she heard the words of it. "They have no need of the sun, neither the moon, to shine in it, for the Lord God giveth them light."

Then she laughed out of her joy, for she knew where she was. And she knew too why she was here, and why she had been born into that life she had left, and why those whom she had loved had been born into it, had suffered in it, and had left it; to reflect and transmit this light from the mirror of a pain-cleansed spirit.

"Who sang to me?" she asked, and there was a flutter of wings above her. A small blue bird was with her, not flinging her snatches of song as she passed like the birds in the trees, but accompanying her all the way that she went with his music and the flutter of his wings. She could not hear the words of his song now, but she had heard them. He had been with her all the time, she was sure, but just at first she had not seen him. As she became more familiar with this country, she knew that as she went on the boundaries of it would widen. It was the glorified beauty of the familiar and habitable earth that she saw now, the trees and flowers and creatures that made up the sweetness of it, but soon she would see more. She would see the spirits of those she loved going about the purposes of

God, bathed in the light of His perpetual compassion; and at the last she would see even further; but of that she dared not think. . . . Yet, thinking of it, she began to run, effortlessly, almost as though she were winged, and the bird, tossing like a blue flame in the air about her, sang and sang and sang.

And then she saw nothing but the darkness of her closed eyes, and with a sickening sense of frustration she knew she was awake. But the bird was still singing; the liquid cascades of his song fell in showers all about her. For a long time she listened, then she opened her eyes and saw him sitting in the ilex tree. . . . But he was only a blackbird after all. . . . For just a moment the blueness of the morning had been reflected in his shining feathers.

Yet how happy she was. One part of her mind was telling her that her dream was just a mix-up of the dawn and the flowers in the garden and the singing blackbird, but another part of it was saying that one would interpenetrate another; we live in them both, but of the greater we know now only that which the lesser tells us of it; and the language of the lesser is the language of dreams and birdsong, sunshine and the kindliness of humanity. [1]

∽

I take Thy hand, and fears grow still;
    Behold Thy face, and doubts remove;
Who would not yield his wavering will
    To perfect truth and boundless love?
                —*Samuel Johnson*

Doubt thou the stars are fire;
    Doubt that the sun doth move;
Doubt truth to be a liar;
    But never doubt I love.
               —*William Shakespeare*

Shakespeare may have been speaking of human love here—but in reality, God's love is the foundation of our lives, the one thing we need never doubt. This love follows us wherever we go, for God is always with us, even when our human eyes can't see Him. He understands our blindness, though, and He gives us bright glimpses of His presence. We can find Him everywhere—in the beauty of nature, in the love of our families, in our dreams, and most of all in His Word. He is our ever-present Companion who will never fail us.

Thou that has given so much to me,
    Give one thing more, a grateful heart.
Not thankful when it pleaseth me,
    As if thy blessings had spare days;
But such a heart, whose pulse may be Thy praise.
               —*George Herbert*

"For I am persuaded, that neither death, nor life, nor angels, nor principalities, nor powers, nor things present, nor things to come, nor height, nor depth, nor any other creature, shall be able to separate us from the love of God, which is in Christ Jesus our Lord."

—Romans 8:38–39

～

Dearest Lord, thank You for Your constant presence. Sharpen my vision so that I may see Your face. Amen.

LOVE'S SERVICE

I should not dare to call my soul my own.
—*Elizabeth Barrett Browning*

∽

If you stop to be kind you must swerve often
from your path.

—*Mary Webb*

∽

"And there came a certain poor widow, and she
threw in two mites, which made a farthing. And he
. . .saith unto them, . . . 'For all they did cast in of
their abundance; but she of her want did cast in all
that she had, even all her living.' "

—*Mark 12:42–44*

∽

*When God has given us so much, we need to
remember to return that love. And as Christ told His
disciples, the way to love Him is by showing our
love concretely to those in need around us. This is
what it means to be His disciple.*

THE TRUE MEANING OF DISCIPLESHIP

"Is it true that the church of today, the church that is called after Christ's own name, would refuse to follow Him at the expense of suffering, of physical loss, of temporary gain? The statement was made last week by a leader of workingmen that it was hopeless to look to the church for any reform or redemption of society. On what was that statement based? Plainly, on the assumption that the church contains for the most part men and women who think more of their own ease and luxury than of the sufferings and needs and sins of humanity. How far is that true? Are the Christians of America ready to have their discipleship tested? . . . How about the men and women of great talent? Are they ready to consecrate that talent to humanity as Jesus undoubtedly would do? . . .

"What is the test of Christian discipleship? Is it not the same as in Christ's own time? Have our surroundings modified or changed the test? If Jesus were here today. . .I believe He would demand—He does demand now—as close a following, as much suffering, as great self-denial as when He lived in person on the earth. . . .

"What would Jesus do? Is not that what the disciple ought to do? Is he not commanded to follow in His steps? How much is the Christianity of the age suffering for Him? . . . What does the age need more than personal sacrifice? . . .

"It is the personal element that Christian discipleship needs to emphasize. 'The gift without the giver is bare.' The Christianity that attempts to suffer by proxy is not the Christianity of Christ. . . . Each individual Christian. . .needs to follow in His steps along the path of personal sacrifice to Him. . . .

"Are we ready to make and live a new discipleship? Are we ready to reconsider our definition of a Christian? What is it to be a Christian? It is to imitate Jesus. It is to do as He would do. It is to walk in His steps." [1]

∽

"Love is patient, love is kind. It does not envy, it does not boast, it is not proud. It is not rude, it is not self-seeking, it is not easily angered, it keeps no record of wrongs. Love does not delight in evil but rejoices with the truth. . .always hopes, always perseveres. Love never fails."

—*1 Corinthians 13:4–8 (NIV)*

∽

Sometimes we think to be good Christians we must act in a certain way, go to a certain church, speak a certain vocabulary. John Wesley reminds us, however, that our love for others is what really matters.

THE HIGHEST GIFT

Love is the highest gift of God; humble, gentle, patient love. All visions, revelations, manifestations, whatever are little things compared to love.

It were well you should be thoroughly sensible of this—the heaven of heavens is love. There is nothing higher in religion; there is, in effect, nothing else. If you look for anything but more love, you are looking wide of the mark, you are getting out of the royal way. . .

Settle it then, in your heart that from the moment God has saved you from all sin, you are to aim at nothing more but more of that love described in the thirteenth chapter of Corinthians. You can go no higher than this until you are carried into Abraham's bosom.

—*John Wesley*

Freely we serve,
Because we freely love.

—*John Milton*

"For this is the message that ye heard from the beginning, that we should love one another. . . . My little children, let us not love in word, neither in tongue; but in deed and in truth."

—*1 John 3:11, 18*

Familiar acts are beautiful through love.
—*Percy Bysshe Shelley*

Even the smallest, most trivial things we do become beautiful when we do them from love. In the following selection, Brother Lawrence echoes Wesley's advice: Love is the only part of our religion that matters. It is what makes our faith alive; and it is what unites us with God.

Doing Little Things for Love

We shouldn't get tired of doing little things for the love of God. God looks not on the size of the job, but on the love with which we do it. We shouldn't be surprised, though, if in the beginning we often failed when we tried to live our life this way—but in the end we will form new habits that will allow us to live our life this way effortlessly and joyfully. . . .

Faith, hope, and love are the only things that matter in religion, and the practice of them unites us with God's will. Everything else is unimportant, merely a bridge to be got across quickly so that we can get to our final destination where we will lose ourselves in faith and love. [2]

He prayeth best who loveth best
    All things both great and small;
For the dear God who loveth us,
    He made and loveth all.
        —Samuel Taylor Coleridge

"Above all, love each other deeply,
because love covers over a multitude of sins."
—*1 Peter 4:8 (NIV)*

$\sim$

In the next selection, Wesley again reminds us of love's vital importance in our lives. Where he speaks of neighbors, remember to insert not only the names of your friends and neighbors, but also your husband's and children's names.

Cover All Things with Love

Seeing thou canst do all things through Christ strengthening thee, be merciful as thy Father in heaven is merciful. Love thy neighbor as thyself. Love friends and enemies as thy own soul; and let thy love be long-suffering and patient. . . .

In love, cover all things. Of the dead and the absent speak nothing but good. Believe all things which may in any way tend to clear your neighbor's character. Hope all things in his favour and endure all things, triumphing over all opposition: for true love never faileth, in time or in eternity.

—*John Wesley*

$\sim$

If I can stop one heart from breaking,
    I shall not live in vain;
If I can ease one life the aching,

Or cool one pain,
Or help one fainting robin
Unto his nest again,
I shall not live in vain.

—Emily Dickinson

∽

"Love is the fulfilling of the law."
—Romans 13:10

∽

Love seeketh not itself to please,
Nor for itself hath any care,
But for another gives its ease,
And builds a Heaven in Hell's despair.

—William Blake

∽

" 'Greater love has no one than this,
that he lay down his life for his friends.' "
—John 15:13 (NIV)

∽

True love makes us reckless. It makes us willing to spend everything we have, even ourselves, for the Christ who loved us so much.

OUR ONLY OCCUPATION

My soul is occupied
> And all my substance in His service. . . .
Nor have I any other employment,
> My sole occupation is love.

Before. . .I was entangled in many useless occupations by which I sought to please myself and others. All this is over now, for all my thoughts, words, and actions are directed to God. All my occupation now is the practice of the love of God. All I do is done in love. [She] who loves God seeks neither gain nor reward, but only to lose all, even [herself].

—*John of the Cross*

$\sim$

For one human being to love another: that is perhaps the most difficult of all our tasks, the ultimate, the last test and proof, the work for which all other work is but preparation.

—*Rainer Maria Rilke*

$\sim$

To love means to communicate to the other, that you will never fail him or let him down when he needs you, but that you will always be standing by with all the necessary encouragements. It is something one can communicate to another only if one has it.

—*Ashley Montagu*

[She] who loves God seeks neither gain nor reward, but only to lose all, even [herself].

—John of the Cross

～

"Beloved, if God so loved us, we ought also to love one another."

—1 John 4:11

～

Dear God, You know how much I love my family. Help me to remember that when I express my love to them, I am also loving You. Remind me to live my life in love's service. Please bring me back when I stray out of this "royal way." I love You, Father. Give me strength to love You more. Amen.

NOTES

GOD'S MIRRORS
1. Sanna, Ellyn. "Mother's Day Meditation." *Marriage & Family,* November 1990.

FLAME-KINDLERS, SEED-PLANTERS, WEALTH-GIVERS
1. Johnson, Joseph. *Willing Hearts and Ready Hands*. T. Nelson & Sons. London: 1870.

2. Alcott, Louisa May. *Little Men*. Nelson Doubleday. Garden City, New York: 1955.

MARRIAGE & LOVE
1. Prentiss, Elizabeth. *Stepping Heavenward*. Barbour Publishing, Inc. Uhrichsville, Ohio: 1998.

2. Sanna, Ellyn. "Married Peace: Forget the Fairy Tales." *Vista: Holy Living Digest,* 12 January 1997.

HOME
1. Sanna, Ellyn, ed. *The Riches of Bunyan*. Barbour Publishing, Inc. Uhrichsville, Ohio: 1998.

2. Sanna, Ellyn. *Motherhood: A Spiritual Journey*. Paulist Press. Mahwah, New Jersey: 1997.

THE FRUSTRATIONS OF DAILY LIFE
1. *Motherhood: A Spiritual Journey.*

2. *Stepping Heavenward.*

3. Smith, Hannah Whitall. *The Christian's Secret of a Happy Life*. Barbour Publishing, Inc. Uhrichsville, Ohio: 1985.

BECOMING COMFORTABLE WITH OURSELVES
1. Goudge, Elizabeth. *The Heart of the Family*. Coward-McCann. New York: 1948.

2. *Stepping Heavenward.*

3. Brother Lawrence. *The Practice of the Presence of God*. Barbour Publishing, Inc. Uhrichsville, Ohio: 1998.

WORRIES
1. *Motherhood: A Spiritual Journey.*

2. Goforth, Rosalind. *How I Know God Answers Prayer.* Zondervan. Grand Rapids, Michigan: 1921.

STRENGTH IN ADVERSITY
1. Sanna, Ellyn. "Safe Am I." *Vista: Holy Living Digest,* 12 October 1997.

OUR HEAVENLY COMPANION
1. Goudge, Elizabeth. *The Bird in the Tree.* Coward-McCann. New York: 1940.

LOVE'S SERVICE
1. Sheldon, Charles M. *In His Steps.* Barbour Publishing Inc. Uhrichsville, Ohio: 1984.

2. *The Practice of the Presence of God.*

Inspirational Library

Beautiful purse/pocket-size editions of Christian classics bound in flexible leatherette. These books make thoughtful gifts for everyone on your list, including yourself!

When I'm on My Knees   The highly popular collection of devotional thoughts on prayer, especially for women.
Flexible Leatherette $4.97

The Bible Promise Book   Over 1,000 promises from God's Word arranged by topic. What does God promise about matters like: Anger, Illness, Jealousy, Love, Money, Old Age, and Mercy? Find out in this book!
Flexible Leatherette $3.97

Daily Wisdom for Women   A daily devotional for women seeking biblical wisdom to apply to their lives. Scripture taken from the New American Standard Version of the Bible.
Flexible Leatherette $4.97

My Daily Prayer Journal   Each page is dated and features a Scripture verse and ample room for you to record your thoughts, prayers, and praises. One page for each day of the year.
Flexible Leatherette $4.97